Recycled!

First published in 2000 by
Franklin Watts
96 Leonard Street
London
EC2A 4XD

Franklin Watts Australia
14 Mars Road
Lane Cove
NSW 2066

A CIP catalogue record for this book is available
from the British Library.

ISBN 0 7496 3727 7

Series Editor: Louise John
Series Advisor: Dr Barrie Wade
Series Designer: Jason Anscomb

Printed in Hong Kong

Recycled!

by Jillian Powell

Illustrated by Amanda Wood

W
FRANKLIN WATTS
NEW YORK • LONDON • SYDNEY

Class 2d was learning all
about recycling.

"Let's start a recycling bank," said Miss Drew.

"We can put it in the
school hall."

7

Some people brought bottles.
Some people brought cans.

Others brought newspapers,
egg boxes or old clothes.

Soon, the recycling bank
was almost full.

"Next week we'll take it to the recycling centre in town," said Miss Drew.

Miss Han was the art teacher.

Next day at Assembly,

she saw all the egg boxes.

"We'll use them to make an alligator," she told Miss Drew.

So she took them back to her classroom.

Mrs Bell, the dinner lady,
saw all the bottles
and jars.

"I'll use these for my jam,"
she told Miss Drew.

So, she took them home
and made lots of jam.

Strawberry Jam

Mr Timms, the headmaster, was moving house.

He needed something to wrap his china in.

"These newspapers are just what I need," he told Miss Drew.

So he used them to wrap
up his china.

Mr Green, the caretaker,
saw the tin cans.

"I know what I can do with these," he told Miss Drew.

Mrs Roberts, the RE teacher, saw the old, woollen clothes.

"These are just what I need," she told Miss Drew.

When 2d came to collect
the rubbish, it had all gone.

"It's all been recycled!" said Miss Drew.

So they started recycling

all over again!

Leapfrog has been specially designed to fit the requirements of the National Literacy Strategy. It offers real books for beginning readers by top authors and illustrators.

There are eleven other Leapfrog stories to choose from:

The Bossy Cockerel   ISBN 0 7946 3708 0
Written by Margaret Nash, illustrated by Elisabeth Moseng

Bill's Baggy Trousers   ISBN 0 7496 3709 9
Written by Susan Gates, illustrated by Anni Axworthy

Mr Spotty's Potty   ISBN 0 7496 3711 0
Written by Hilary Robinson, illustrated by Peter Utton

Little Joe's Big Race   ISBN 0 7496 3712 9
Written by Andy Blackford, illustrated by Tim Archbold

The Little Star   ISBN 0 7496 3713 7
Written by Deborah Nash, illustrated by Richard Morgan

The Cheeky Monkey   ISBN 0 7946 3710 2
Written by Anne Cassidy, illustrated by Lisa Smith

Selfish Sophie   ISBN 0 7496 3726 9
Written by Damian Kelleher, illustrated by Georgie Birkett

Pippa and Poppa   ISBN 0 7496 3727 7
Written by Anne Cassidy, illustrated by Philip Norman

Felix on the Move   ISBN 0 7496 3731 5
Written by Maeve Friel, illustrated by Beccy Blake

The Best Snowman   ISBN 0 7496 3728 5
Written by Margaret Nash, illustrated by Jörg Saupe

Jack's Party   ISBN 0 7496 3730 7
Written by Ann Bryant, illustrated by Claire Henley